W9-ADH-314

DEIRDRE LANGELAND

illustrated by

SARAH MAI

CLARION BOOKS

Imprints of HarperCollins*Publishers*

FOR FREDDIE SPAGHETTI
—D.L.

TO LINDA AND DAVE,
THE COOLEST PEOPLE I KNOW
—S.M.

Clarion Books is an imprint of HarperCollins Publishers.
HarperAlley is an imprint of HarperCollins Publishers.

The Cool Code

www.harperalley.com

Library of Congress Control Number: 2022935798
ISBN 978-0-35-854932-1 (hardcover)
ISBN 978-0-35-854931-4 (paperback)

The artist used ProCreate to create the digital illustrations for this book.
Lettering by Whitney Leader-Picone and Natalie Fondriest

22 23 24 25 26 GPS 10 9 8 7 6 5 4 3 2 1
❖
First Edition

SOMETIMES, I WISH EVERYTHING COULD BE AS SIMPLE AS PROGRAMMING. ON THE COMPUTER, YOU CAN MAKE ANYTHING HAPPEN. YOU JUST HAVE TO WRITE THE CODE. IT DOESN'T WORK OUT HOW YOU WANT IT? GO BACK AND FIX IT.

TAP TAP TAP TAP TAP TAP TAP TAP TAP TAP TAP TAP TAP TAP

IN REAL LIFE, THERE ARE NO DO-OVERS.

Turn on a light, Zoey. I swear you'll ruin your eyes before you turn 13.
FUR-BULOUS
TAP TAP TAP TAP TAP TAP
I *already* wear glasses.
CLICK
You just have no appreciation for a good moody moment.
REMEMBER...
be cool.

That may be true. But it's still time to stop coding. Dinner is ready.
Okay, I'll be there in a minute.
Don't forget to wash your hands!
SIGH
STRETCH
IN A LOT OF WAYS, I'M PRETTY MUCH LIKE ANY OTHER KID. I MEAN, YOU PROBABLY WOULDN'T LOOK TWICE IF YOU PASSED ME IN THE STREET.
BUT THERE IS ONE THING ABOUT ME THAT'S KIND OF DIFFERENT: I DON'T HAVE A LOT OF FRIENDS. IN FACT, I DON'T REALLY HAVE *ANY*.
DOES THAT MAKE ME SOUND WEIRD?

MUNCH
MUNCH
MUNCH
CHOMP
CHOMP
Are you ready for tomorrow?
GLUG
GLUG
Ummm, let me think on that...
Nope. Definitely not.

I know starting a new school is stressful, but it's going to be fine, Zonut. Really.
Easy for you to say. You're going to be here with Mom all day! I'm the one who's getting thrown to the wolves.
CHOMP CHOMP
I'm joking.
Well...maybe not entirely. But I'm definitely exaggerating.
I'll be fine...
I have a few tricks up my sleeve.

I'VE BEEN HOMESCHOOLED MY WHOLE LIFE, SO I JUST NEVER HUNG OUT WITH A LOT OF KIDS. BUT THEN THIS YEAR...IN THE MIDDLE OF ***OCTOBER***...

...MY PARENTS DECIDED TO SEND ME TO SCHOOL. I WAS WORRIED ABOUT FITTING IN, BUT THEN I REALIZED, I HAVE A SECRET WEAPON...

...COMPUTER PROGRAMMING. I CAN CODE MY WAY OUT OF PRETTY MUCH ANY PROBLEM. WHY NOT THIS?

COOL CODE

SWIPE TO UNLOCK

SWIPE

COOL CODE

CLICK

Welcome to the Cool Code! Who are you going to impress today? Select a scenario from the menu below.

SEE? EASY-PEASY.

PARTY
DOCTOR'S OFFICE
NEW SCHOOL
DANCE-OFF
You have selected "New School." The Cool Code app can help. Let's begin by planning your outfit.
Please select the date that you will be entering your new school.
TAP TAP TAP TAP TAP TAP TAP TAP TAP
ASSESSING CLOSET INVENTORY...
OUTFIT IDENTIFIED

Based on your social situation and weather forecasts for your area, the Cool Code suggests... a skirt and tights.
Really? I was thinking maybe leggings would–
The Cool Code is based on algorithms that *you* programmed, remember?
The green one!

Okay, okay... You're right.
No second-guessing.
Sleep tight, Zo... Tomorrow's a big day!
CLICK

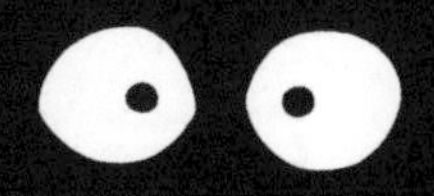

CHAPTER 2
REMEMBER...
STICK TO THE CODE!!!
Ready, Zoey?
Ready as I'll ever be, I guess...
You *guess?* I'm a state-of-the-art program. They'll be falling all over you before you get to homeroom.
Yeah, yeah...

You look like a million bucks. Now, let's get going before we get stuck in traffic.
Are you suuuure this is a good idea, Dad? I mean, how can a school possibly be as good as you and Mom?
We've been over this, Zo. Hawthorne is an excellent school.
What if all the stuff you taught me is different from what they learn at school?
Zoey, you placed a grade above your age level. You'll do fine.
But what if *I'm* different?

HAWTHORNE MIDDLE SCHOOL
Have a great day, Zonut!
HERE GOES NOTHING.

GULP
Okay, C.C.
How do I find my
first class without
looking like an
idiot?

What are you doing? Phones aren't allowed in school.
Oh, I didn't know. It's just an app.
Uh... Never mind. I'm Zoey—I'm new.
That's obvious.

GULP
So–
The office is down the hall on your right.
SLUMP

POW
The Cool Code is here to help. Who do you need to impress?
Uh, EVERYBODY!!! I've only been here for 30 seconds and I feel like this whole plan is already FALLING APART!!
The Cool Code recommends that you take a deep breath.
Close your eyes. Breathe in through your nose and out through your mouth.

Ha. Yeah. Okay.
That was actually really good advice. Maybe this is gonna work...
Well, of course it's going to work! You programmed me, didn't you?
Well, yes. But–
And you're the best 12-year-old coder around, right?
Yeah, I kind of am.
So here's what you're going to do: get out of this bathroom and go kick some middle school butt.
YES!
Don't worry, I've got your back...

MAIN OFFICE
OCT 14 8:24AM
OCTOBER
Can I help you with something?
Yeah—my name is Zoey McIntyre. I'm new, and I need my homeroom assignment.
Okay, yeah. You're in Mr. Watson's class.
That's just down the hall. I'll give you directions.
Or I could show you how to get there?
C.C.... what now?

...C.C.?
The Cool Code has unexpectedly quit. Please reboot and try again.
C.C.? You're supposed to be backing me up here!
Ahem.
Ummm...it would be great if you could show me how to get there.
No problem... I'm Daniel, by the way.
Thanks, Daniel! These halls are kinda confusing...

Do you always work in the office? Aren't you a student?
I'm in eighth grade. I only volunteer there during homeroom.
Me too! I mean, I'm in eighth grade too.
I know.
You do?
Yeah. I looked up your homeroom, remember?
Oh, right. Haha.

So...do you always talk to your pocket?
Ha! Only when it talks to me first!
Okay, so it looks like your locker is 108.
MR WATSON'S CLASSROOM
202
Here's your locker, and your homeroom is right there.

Thanks. Really. I never would've found this on my own.
No problem. It was cool meeting you, Zoey.
THE PROBLEM WITH PROGRAMMING IS THAT IT'S EASY TO FORGET THAT NO AMOUNT OF PLANNING CAN EVER REALLY PREPARE YOU FOR STUFF IN THE REAL WORLD.

Hmm...
Looks like
Mr. Watson isn't
here yet.
Hey,
y'all...
HELLO!!!!
EVERYONE!!!!

AHEM
This is Zoey. She's new. Maybe someone could show her to her next class after this period?
Well, I have to get back to the office.

Don't worry—you'll get the hang of it!
Is that desk taken?
EXCUSE ME! IS THIS DESK TAKEN?
GULP

FIRST PERIOD
BRRIING
Hi! Can you tell me where–
Excuse me!
AARRGGH!
BRRRIIINNG

SECOND PERIOD
FORMULAS
3n + 2 = 17
3n + 2 - 2 = 17 - 2
3n/3 = 15/3
n =
BRRIIING
HUFF
HUFF
Um...is this the eighth-grade science classroom?
Nope. Sorry.
WELCOME
This Week:

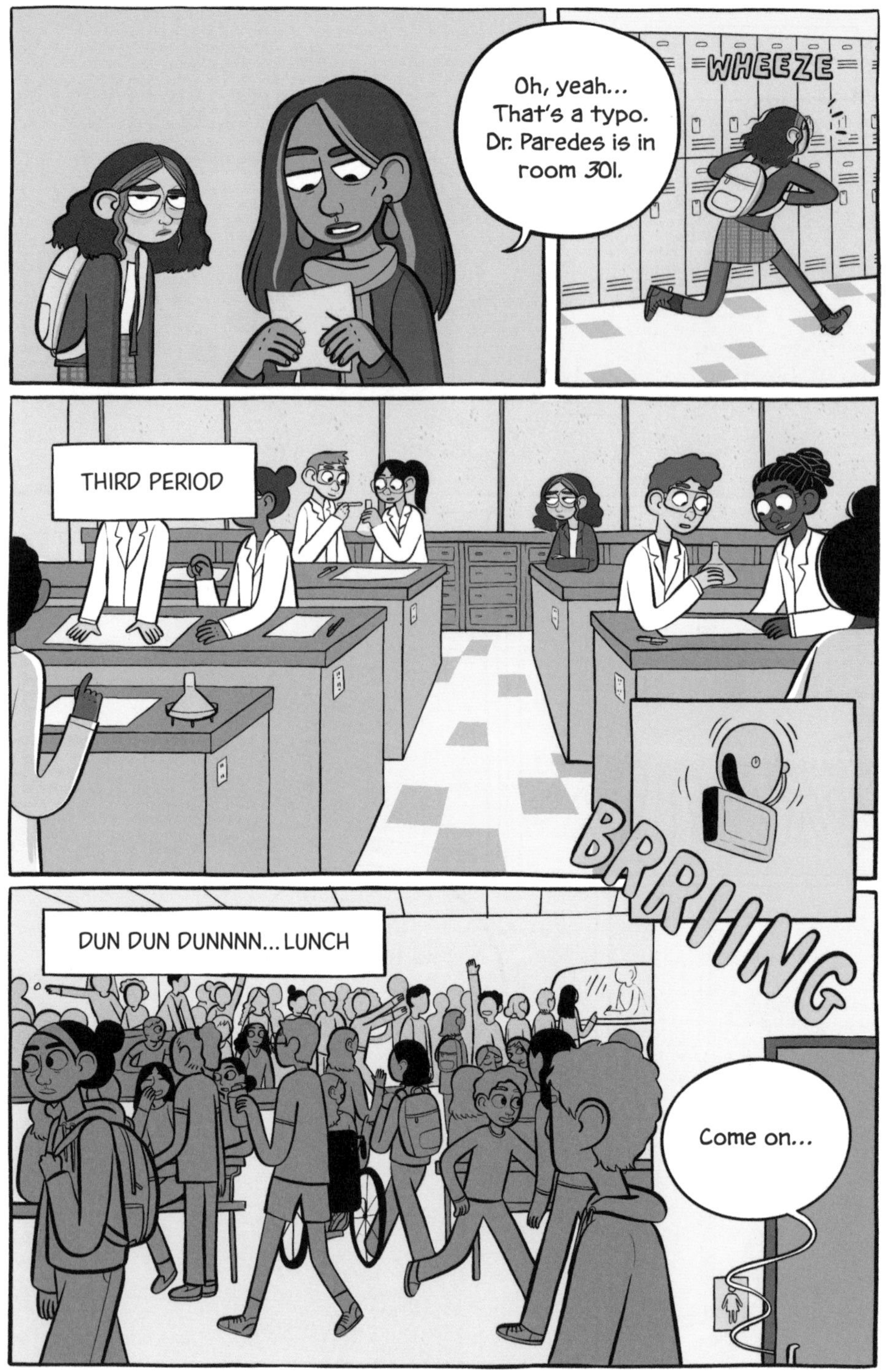
Oh, yeah... That's a typo. Dr. Paredes is in room 301.
WHEEZE
THIRD PERIOD
BRRIING
DUN DUN DUNNNN... LUNCH
Come on...

Reboot, already!
Welcome to the Cool Code! Who are you going to impress today? Select a scenario from the menu below.
I needed to impress them three hours ago, but whatever.
TAP TAP TAP TAP
POP!
The Cool Code has been shut down incorrectly. Would you like to file a report?
I'll tell myself all about it later.

Right now, you have serious work to do. It's lunchtime.
Lunchtime? I eat lunchtime for lunch!
I guess I need to work on some of your phrases...
POOF!
Online data suggests that locally sourced farm-to-table cuisine is the coolest. Look for gently poached eggs on a bed of wilted chard.

Somehow, I don't think that's going to be an option.
Okay, how about certified humane food?
Try again.
Do you need help finding something? The rolls are vegan if that's what you're looking for.
Actually, a vegan diet is pretty cool. It's not at the top of the rankings, but you can eat it.

I'm not sure it's cool to eat that much of *anything.*
Hey—I'm hungry. If I have to eat carrots, at least I'm going to fill up.
Just don't mess up this part. Everybody's going to be watching you.
Don't hesitate. Head straight for the nearest empty seat.
Okay... How about that one?
I SAID, DON'T HESITATE!!!

Smooth move. You know I'm an app, not a fairy godmother, right? There's only so much I can fix.
Are you okay?
Yeah. Thanks. I guess I was so busy looking for a seat, I didn't see that backpack.
We can make room for you at my table.
Assessing new contact.

Where is that coming from? Is that your phone again?
Heh. Yeah—I think I forgot to turn off my alarm. Let me hit the silent switch.
CLICK
SUBJECT NAME:
UNKNOWN
CLOTHING:
MODERATELY COOL
INTERACTION STYLE:
ABOVE AVERAGE
PRELIMINARY COOL ASSESSMENT:
GOOD
POP!
Hey, y'all! This is Zoey. She just started at Hawthorne.
Hey!
Zoey, this is Caitlyn and her brother, Adam.

And that's Morgan.
How come?
Excuse me?
I think he *meant* to say, "Hi."
Hi.
How come you're starting in the middle of the year? Did you move or something?
Oh! No...
I've lived here my whole life. I've just been homeschooled until now.

Wait. So you've *never* been to school before?
This is my first day of school. Ever.
Whoa! That's totally wild. I mean, awesome. It's cool. Really.
RUMBLE
Ummm... are you hungry? Do you want some of my fries?
Oh. No, thanks. I'm...uh... a vegan?

The french fries are vegan.
Really? Thanks! I'd love some!
MUNCH MUNCH MUNCH
So, if you've been homeschooled for so long, why the sudden change?
SHRUG
Now that my classes are getting more complicated, my parents think I'm better off with specialized teachers.

Plus, they're starting up their own company, so they're going to be too busy to teach me for a while.
So here I am. Honestly, it's a little overwhelming. Everything moves so–
BRRRRRRRIIIINNGGG
...fast.

CHAMPIONS
FOURTH PERIOD
BONK
FIFTH PERIOD
LORD OF THE FLIES GROUP DISCUSSION
READ FOR FUN!
SIXTH PERIOD

2:45 P.M.
Zoey!
So? How was your first-ever day of school?
It was...
I mean...
It was...

So HARD!
There are so many kids and so many classes. You never have time to just think.
Why don't they give you more time in between classes? Why is lunch so short? How am I supposed to keep all this straight??
PANT PANT
So...
not great, then?
Zonut...
It won't always be this tough. You're just figuring things out.

Give it a couple of weeks and I promise you, things are going to look a lot better.
A couple of *weeks*? Another *day* of that and I'm going to have a nervous breakdown!
I'm going to do some work.
Homework on the first day, huh?
Not much. Mostly I need to work on my app.
Oh, yes... the secret app. How's that going?
Not so great. It's pretty buggy.

I can help you with that, if you want. Maybe after dinner?
Thanks, but I think I'd rather keep the secret app...you know...*secret.*
I THOUGHT I HAD IT ALL FIGURED OUT. WHAT A JOKE.
BUT NOBODY GETS A PROGRAM EXACTLY RIGHT ON THEIR FIRST TRY. THAT'S WHY DEBUGGING IS A BIG PART OF PROGRAMMING. YOU HAVE TO SEE HOW IT REACTS TO USER INPUT.
REMEMBER...
BREATHE

ERROR REPORT
10.10.2 :45 AM
UNEXPE TDOWN

THE CODING PART IS STRAIGHTFORWARD, BUT PEOPLE AREN'T. YOU CAN'T PLAN FOR EVERYTHING THEY MIGHT DO.

TAP TAP TAP TAP TAP TAP TAP TAP TAP TAP TAP TAP

IF THINGS DON'T GO HOW YOU WANT THEM TO, YOU TWEAK THE PROGRAM. THEN YOU TRY IT AGAIN.

TAP TAP TAP TAP TA TAP TAP TAP T

Zoey, it's like a cave in there. Turn on a light!

CLICK

CHAPTER 3
6:30
WAKE UP!
BEEP BEEP BEEP BEEP BEEP BEEP
Beep! Beep! Beep!
Beep, beep! It's 6:30 a.m.!
Time to get you cleaned up...
REMEMBER...
BREATHE
BLOOMING
This could take a while.
What?

Use the unscented soap! Not that really smelly flowery one that your mother likes!
You're wearing *that*? You might as well just switch me off right now.
Steady...steady...
THAT'S TOO MUCH!!

SEE? JUST TWEAK THE PROGRAM AND RUN IT AGAIN.
Let's do this!
Knock 'em dead, Zonut!
Bye, Dad!
He *cannot* call you that in front of other people...

Okay, step one: head for your locker.
Unload all your books and your backpack. Only carry the absolute minimum.
This is it? You're going to have to do some decorating. It should scream personality in here.
BRRIIIINNGG
SLAM
Oh NO!

Whoa, Nelly!
Sloooow doooown!!!
PANT PANT
Cool kids do *not* run to class. Take it slow.
Slowwwwerrrrrrr.
HUFF HUFF

See? No problem. You made it.
Hi! Sorry, I–
Don't apologize.
RECYCLING RULES!
Oh! Okay, ummm...
Shhhhhh! Just sit down.
SCIENCE CLUB!
HOW TO GROW A PLANT
See? No one even noticed you came in.
Hey, you're right! But don't I want people to notice me?
Well, sure, when you're doing something cool.
Not when you're sweaty and out of breath. You look like you just crawled out of a rain forest.
Hey!

What?
What?
You just said something.
I did?
Yeah. You said, "Hey!"
Oh. Yeah. I was talking to myself. Sorry...
Okay...
Did you just come from the gym or something?
Told you so.

FIRST PERIOD
ARTICLE I
BLAH BLAH BLAH BLAH BLAH
I got this.
Audio capture *on!*
BRRIIINNGG
THIRD PERIOD
It looks like someone is out sick.

Hey! Is your partner absent?
Yeah... looks like it.
Want to work together?
YEP. COOL LOGIC AND CAREFUL PLANNING CAN ALWAYS CUT THROUGH THE CHAOS.
Wow! We're *crushing* it today.
Yeah! I just needed a couple of bugs fixed. Next stop: Popular Town!
What's with the new girl?
Just weird, I guess. She's been talking to herself all morning.

See those kids over there?
The two by the lockers?
Yeah. Walk over there and introduce yourself.
What? Aren't there rules about that kind of thing?
The rules in middle school are the same as everywhere else. Just walk over, shake their hands, and say, "Hi, my name is Zoey."
I don't know about this...
Have I steered you wrong?
Not *today*...

Hi, my name is Zoey.
Hi! How are you? My name is Zoey.
Definitely weird.
Okay, that was my bad.
It's *possible* that I might need more data on middle school social customs.
HEHEHEHEHE

Ya think?
You know, maybe I'll take it from here.
CLICK
COOL CODE
SHUTTING DOWN
That seems fair.
POP!

BACK AT HOME...
How's the homework going?
Okay. It's not too hard.
That's good. It's weird to see you doing work I didn't assign.
It's kind of weird learning from other teachers.

Was school better today?
It started out okay. I really felt like I was starting to get the hang of things...
But then everything kind of went haywire.
I just don't feel like I fit in at all.
Listen, Zonut. You're the most lovable kid I've ever met. You just need to show everyone who you are and they'll love you as much as I do.
No offense, Dad, but that's the *worst* advice. You're my dad. You *have* to love me.
And you can't call me Zonut in front of any kids from school, okay? I'll never fit in if they find out I was nicknamed after a breakfast food.
Okay, well, I don't want to add to your woes, but I have an important conference call tomorrow. You're going to have to take the bus to school.
COUGH
WHAT?!

I know you were hoping we could drive you for a while longer, but it's just not workable.
But–
Things are really starting to ramp up with the business. Mom and I just can't spare the time to drive you back and forth to school.
DAD! I'm trying to convince the kids at school that I'm *cool*. There's nothing *less* cool than riding the bus!!
I'm sorry, Zonut, but you're just going to have to figure out another way to convince the Hawthorne kids of your awesomeness.
It's not Zonut. It's *Zo*.

The *bus*?
REMEMBER...
NOTHING IS FAIR
You'll need a strategy to manage this. I would recommend a disguise.
MOAN
FLOP
Dad thinks I should just suck it up and let everyone see the real me.
FLOP
Huh. That's kind of interesting.
No, it's not.
Yeah, you're probably right. After all, your best friend right now is an app.
A *glitchy* app. Let's see if we can figure out what's wrong with you.
TAP TAP TAP TAP
TAP

COMPUTER CODE IS KIND OF LIKE LEGOS. WHEN YOU FOCUS ON THE INDIVIDUAL PIECES, YOU CAN'T SEE THE COMPLETE PROGRAM. BUT STEP BACK AND LOOK AT THE WHOLE PROJECT AND YOU CAN SEE WHAT YOU'VE BUILT: IT'S A CASTLE OR A PIRATE SHIP OR SOMETHING.

SOMETIMES, AFTER YOU'VE GOT EVERYTHING IRONED OUT, THE SCENARIO CHANGES. THEN YOU HAVE TO RETOOL YOUR PROGRAM TO FILL A DIFFERENT FUNCTION. SO YOU SHUFFLE THE PIECES AND YOU ADD SOME NEW ONES. SUDDENLY YOUR CASTLE HAS TURNED INTO THE DEATH STAR.

OF COURSE, SOMETIMES RETOOLING WORKS BETTER THAN OTHERS.
Okay, C.C. What now? Should I try to get someone to sit with me?
What's the point? We're already riding the bus. Who's gonna take us seriously now?
But all these kids are on the bus too.
Hey...you're right!
Make eye contact. Smile!

Rejected by the bus kids. You might as well just power me down.
SLIDE

TAP TAP TAP TAP TAP TAP TA
Okay if I sit here?
Sure!

TAP TAP TAP TAP TAP TAP
This must be weird for you.
What must be?
Riding the bus.
Why? Because I'm too cool for the bus?
Haha! No, I mean... I'm sure you *are* too cool for the bus. But have you ever ridden on a school bus before?

Oh. No. I haven't. It's kind of...uncomfortable. Why are these seats so hard?
I hear they make them hard on purpose so you'll appreciate the desk chairs.
That's ridiculous.
Yeah. You're right.
It's probably just cheaper to make 'em this way.
What are you working on?
I'm just coding...
It's an app I've been working on. It's kind of a life guide that gives advice.

That sounds pretty cool.
It *would* be, but I'm having a lot of trouble with it. It's giving some wild answers.
Still...your own app. That's pretty hard-core! You must be a really good programmer.
Pretty good. My parents are both programmers, so it was a big part of my homeschooling.
You know, you could join Coding Club. I'm the president.
Have you already had a lot of meetings? I mean, would it be weird for me to join now?
No! You'll fit right in.
It's a small club. We only have six members.

Okay, to be honest, a lot of them don't show up to the meetings. It's sometimes just Morgan and me.
No... that's not really true. It's pretty much *always* just Morgan and me. Honestly, we could really use you.
Right, Morgan?
I guess she can't hear me with her headphones on.
Anyway, we're meeting after school. Are you in?
Yeah, okay!

2:45 P.M.
ZOEY
Now, *this* looks like a locker that belongs to someone interesting.
If you say so. I think it looks more like a locker that a party supply store threw up in.
You have to trust the process, Zoey.
SLAM
That's getting harder and harder to do...
Hi, Zoey!

Oh! Hi, guys! I was just talking...
I guess I must look like a total weirdo, talking to myself so much.
Nah. That's not a big deal. I talk to myself all the time.
He really does. When he's not blabbing at someone else, he's blah-blah-blahing to himself.
I guess a lot of people talk to themselves. But I'm not... Not really.
I'm talking to my pocket.

I mean, my phone... I'm talking to my phone.
Oooookay... wellll...
We really have to go. We don't want to miss the bus!
CLICK
3:00
That went well.

TODAY IS:
OCTOBER 16 TH
CODING CLUB
LOG IN:
LOG OFF
THINK BEFORE YOU CLICK
THE LAB IS FAB!
LAB RULES

You came! That's so great!
You remember Morgan?
Hey.
So what's so great about you?
Uhhh...
Morgan. Why don't you start with something easier, like "hello"?
'Cause I want to know what's so great about the new kid that everyone's so excited to have her in the club.
If by "everyone," you mean me and Ms. Emberly...
CODING
That's Ms. Emberly, by the way, our faculty advisor.

CODING CLUB
Hi, Zoey. We're *so* excited to have you in the club.
She's a really good programmer. Show her your app, Zoey.
It's not finish—
You haven't even *seen* this thing, Daniel?
Jeez, Morgan. Calm down. We could use some new members.
I'm starting to see why no one comes to your meetings.

Why don't we start over? Zoey, this is Morgan. She started the club with me when we were in sixth grade. She's really cool once you get to know her.
Hmph.
Morgan, this is Zoey. She just started at Hawthorne. Both her parents are programmers, and she's pretty good at this stuff.
Really? Huh.
So—
What kind of programming do your parents do? Where do they work?

At home, actually. They're starting a new company.
Like, a software company?
Yeah. My mom started working on her own stuff at home. She developed some new encryption technology, and—
Encryption? Like, spy stuff?
Okay— that's kind of cool.
She can stay.
Oh, good. I was really worried you wouldn't approve...
So. How about we get down to club business?

We need to pick our big project for the semester. We're already weeks behind.
That's because everything you've come up with is a snooze fest.
All right, what ideas do *you* have?
How about we program a giant robot and take over the world?
HEHE
Okay, so you don't have any ideas.
Which means we should stick with mine. The PTA could really use a new database to help manage their student and member info.
Couldn't we do that in, like, five minutes with existing software?
Yeeeessssss. But if we built it from the ground up, we'd learn more.
And we could design a cool user interface so they could create directories and parents could log on to access the information and make updates...

See what I mean?
Um, yeah. A little... But if there are no other ideas...
Are you kidding me, new girl? Just because we have no other ideas doesn't mean we should do the most pointless, tedious thing we can think of!
WHACK
Is she always like this?
Yep. Pretty much.
HEY! I'm right here.
And I am NOT building a PTA database from scratch!

Okay, fine.
Let's all bring some new, *realistic* ideas to next week's meeting.
Okay?
Hmmpph.
TODAY IS:
OCTOBER 16TH
CODING CLUB
LOG IN:
LOG OFF
THINK BEFORE YOU CLICK
THE LAB IS FAB!
LAB RULES
Moving on, then...

THAT NIGHT...
How was school today, Zo?
Okay. I went to Coding Club after school.
OH! How was it?
It was pretty cool, I guess. I think it will be fun.
See...this is what I was talking about. You just have to be yourself. Pursue your passions!
Okay...
Calm down, Andrew.
Your dad's just proud of you, honey. We are really happy that you're fitting in so well at Hawthorne.

SPUTTER
COUGH

I'm not sure I'd call it *fitting in*, exactly...
Maybe *getting by?*
That's my girl!
Your mom and I have to finish our presentation for tomorrow. Can you serve yourself dessert?
SMEK
What a trouper!

WHEN YOU'RE PUTTING TOGETHER A BIG PROGRAM, YOU REALLY NEED TO CONCENTRATE. THAT CAN TRANSLATE INTO A LOT OF HOURS BY YOURSELF. MY PARENTS ARE LUCKY—THEY'VE FIGURED OUT A WAY TO WORK TOGETHER.
REMEMBER...
you are not alone
FOR THE REST OF US, CODING CAN BE LONELY WORK.

TAP TAP TAP TAP TAP TAP
TAP TAP TAP TAP TAP TAP TAP
TAP
TAP TAP TAP TAP TAP TAP
CLICK
UN-
SIGH

ONE WEEK LATER
CHAPTER 5
OF COURSE, ONCE YOU'VE GOTTEN A PROGRAM UP AND RUNNING, THERE ARE ALWAYS BUGS THAT NEED TO BE FIXED. UPDATES THAT NEED TO BE MADE.
A PROGRAMMER'S JOB IS TO KEEP LOOKING FOR THOSE FLAWS.
CLICK
BUT EVERYONE WANTS THEIR WORK TO SUCCEED, SO IT CAN BE TEMPTING TO OVERLOOK THEM.

TANYA MALDONADO
CLOTHING: EXTREMELY COOL
INTERACTION STYLE: EXCEPTIONAL
PRELIMINARY COOL ASSESSMENT: EXCELLENT
I DON'T KNOW. I GUESS EVERYONE NEEDS COMPANY.
EVEN IF THAT COMPANY ISN'T REAL.

ZZZZZZ
BRRIIING
Wha-? Where?
You were sleeping. The program was reactivated when I started moving.
Okay, I'm ready. Who are we trying to impress?
I don't think I need you for this one.
CLICK

What was that?
What was what?
What were you doing with your phone?
Oh, that! I was just switching it off so it wouldn't go off during our meeting.
You've been talking to that phone all day.
Hi, y'all!
Is that your secret app?
What's up? Is everything okay?
If it *is*, then it's none of your business. That's what *secret* means.
Whoa. What did I miss?
Zoey's doing something on her phone that she's hiding from us.
I'm not hiding it from anybody. I just turned it off so it wouldn't interrupt the meeting.

So then you wouldn't mind showing it to us.
Actually, I would.
Morgan, Zoey's app is none of our business. Can we just have a meeting?
No, we can't. What if she's recording us? That's an invasion of our privacy.
Ms. Emberly!
ARGGH! It's the Cool Code, okay?!
What?

It's an app that analyzes social situations and tells you the best response.
To... you know... be cool.
Really?
It's kind of embarrassing, okay? So I'm keeping it secret.
Okay, Morgan? Can we go on with the meeting now?
No way.
Because...that's *brilliant.* You're telling me there's an app that can make sense out of *middle school*?
Not really. It doesn't really wor–
This could revolutionize the *world.* Think of the millions of kids whose lives could change!

I think that might be a bit of an exaggeration, Morgan.
No. It's not. Middle school is a seething cesspool of angst. Cliques and clubs, cool kids and bullies...
That's not really—
This app could save all the regular kids from a lifetime of trauma.
I think you've been watching too many movies.
You just don't know about it because everybody likes you.
Not *everybody.*
This is a solution to a problem that doesn't exist. Really, *everybody's* just trying to fit in. If you'd just chill out and be nice to people, they'd respond.
Anyway, it doesn't matter. The app doesn't work like it's supposed to. I get these weird responses and I wind up looking like a total idiot.

So? Let's *make* it work!
I don't think—
This is it! This is our big project. We'll fix Zoey's app. For the good of middle schoolers everywhere!
Zoey?
What do you think?
You know what? Yes!
I can't figure it out on my own... Maybe you guys can help.
Daniel?
All right. If you guys want to do this, I'm in.
YES!

Okay, Zoey. Tell me everything.
This is the user interface.
LOG IN
NEW U
CLICK
PLEASE ENTER A USERNAME:
COD_
TAP TAP TAP TAP
WELCOME
Welcome, Coding Club! Before you know it, you're going to be so cool you'll need earmuffs.

Seriously?
Ummm...yeah. It seemed funny at the time?
ADDRESS:
BIRTH DA
ZIP CODE:
Please enter your information.
PRONOUNS:
SCHOOL:
GRAD
When you first fire up the app, you upload information—stuff like your zip code, your pronouns, and your age.
Okay. Cool.
But there's also more specialized information.
Whoa. That's really specific.
PHOBIAS:
PUBLIC SPEAKING
SPIDERS
ENCLOSED SPACES
RACCOONS
HEIGHTS
NOSE PICKER?
YES
NO
Well, the more data the program has, the better it should be at making predictions.

Once you've filled in the basic stuff, you can add in some more advanced data.
CLICK
SETTINGS
ADVANCED
BUILD YOUR WARDROBE
UPDATE YOUR SKILLS
USER INFO
You can upload pictures of all your clothes. Then the app can check the weather using your zip code and coordinate outfits for you.
Really? Wow. Can I try it?
Sure.
As you take pictures, the app will compare each item to clothing in online fashion catalogs and analyze how cool the item is.

NEW ITEM:
DRESS
LONG SLEEVED
MINI-LENGTH
You have one item in your closet inventory. The Cool Code recommends that you burn it immediately.
Ummm... whoops? Sorry.
Yeah, so, the program works pretty much like this:
Welcome to the Cool Code!
You log in, and you can select from a list of scenarios.
Welcome
COOL CODE
LOG IN
Who's that?
That's C.C. He's a llama.
"C.C." is for Cool Code—I know it's kind of weird, but I just started calling him that and then I got used to it.

I'm not too thrilled about it either, Bub.
Whoa! He's voice-activated?
Yeah. The app has two modes. "Planning mode" makes suggestions to help you get ready for whatever it is you want to do.
ENGLISH
SELECT MODE:
PLANNING
ROAMING
DATA PREFERENCE:
CONNECT TO WIFI
USE CELL DATA
In "roaming mode," you leave the app on. It collects data as you go through your day, analyzes it, and then tells you what to do to be cool.
Zoey. This is *really* advanced programming.
PLANNING
ROAMING
You bet your butt. I'm as good as it gets.

You're forgetting that it doesn't work.
Yet. It doesn't work yet.
Excuse me?
COOL ASSESSMENT
PING!

SUBJECT NAME:
UNKNOWN
CLOTHING:
BELOW AVERAGE
INTERACTION STYLE:
ABYSMAL
PRELIMINARY COOL ASSESSMENT:
POOR
ERK
CLICK
Right. So where do we start?
Let's think about it overnight. We can meet again tomorrow and come up with a plan.

CHAPTER 6
BRIGHT AND EARLY THE NEXT MORNING
Hey, Zoey. Have a seat!
I figured I should watch C.C. in action today. I'll be your shadow.
Okay by you?
Okay by me!

Let's see what this thing's got.
Here goes...
CLICK
Whoa! Hey! I'm up! Where are we?
We're in the hallway at school—classes haven't started yet.

What'd I miss?
Her again?
That's Morgan—you can ignore her.
Not the most flattering thing anyone's said about me...
No problem. Ignore input from girl in outmoded frilly skirt.
Hey!

Assessing...
Sorry.
Okay, you really should've let me pick out your outfit today. Take that headband off and put your hair in a ponytail.
I don't have a hair tie!
Then just take the headband off.
And tie that sweater around your waist. Don't *ever* wear it again.
Wow. At least it's not just me...
STUDENT COUNCIL!
What on *earth* made you wear those shoes??

2:45 P.M.
So, C.C. gave some pretty good advice today...
He kept you from coming out of the gym when the cheerleaders were running by. That would've been an epic collision.
He found us a pretty sweet seat at lunch.
BONK
And he got us onto the winning team for dodgeball.

But he also told us to wait outside the boys' bathroom to make friends.
And there is no excuse for what he did to my locker.
Don't forget the banana incident!!

He suggested I yell out "Banana!" during Algebra.
I believed the situation called for some levity...
And you *did* it?
NO!
He did it instead. I have to do detention during lunch on Monday.
Nobody's perfect.
Can we turn C.C. off? I'm having a hard time concentrating with him piping up all the time.
Sorry.
No problem, pal. I'm just a bundle of algorithms.
So, the app gathers data almost perfectly and it processes smoothly.
It's pretty amazing, Zoey. It was even right about your sweater.
POP

Thanks...I think. But it still gives some pretty bad advice.
And you have *got* to stop talking to yourself around school. It's weird.
That's easy to fix. But the wrong answers are a real problem. How did C.C. get his background info?
I mostly gave him a bunch of keywords to run down on the internet.
So you're thinking he needs better data?
Yeah. I think we've been thinking of him like he's a bot—
...but he should be learning like AI!!!
Of course! He needs more than just data. He needs to see cause and effect. He needs *stories.*
Zoey, he can accept feedback and learn, right?
Sure. He processes all kinds of data.
Scientists can spend years training AI before it's ready to be released. C.C. needs to learn nuance. He's just not ready yet.
That makes sense. So what do we do about it?

We need to do *a lot* more research.
Ugh. Research.
Okay, here's the plan: We cram some culture. Movies, books—anything that might teach him more about human behavior.
But he also needs feedback. So he knows what makes sense and what doesn't.
Does that sound right?
I guess. When he suggests something bonkers, I usually just switch him off.
So we'll take him out and give him feedback. Lots and *lots* of feedback.
This might actually work...
Yeah, it will. This is a great plan.
So we start this weekend?
Phase one: research commences tomorrow!

CHAPTER 7
PING!
MMMMMMMMM
MS
DT
you up?
7:37 am
MS

GROAN
PING!
7:37 am
MS
DT
you up?
ITS 7:30 !!!!!!
so?
ITS SATURDAY!!!!!!
gotta save the world
later
What'd I miss?
time to work!
Never text me before 10 on Saturday.
zzz

YOU'RE PURRFECT!
UN-BEE-ABLE
YAWN
CRUNCH
CRUNCH
PING!
before 10 on Saturday.
DT
Zzz
ZM
MS
now?
K
MS
...
meet me at the library in 20.
MS
GROAN

I'm going to the library!
Bye, hon!
ORNE COMMUNITY LIBRARY

FINALLY! What took you so long?
I got here as fast as I cou—
Never mind. We have *so* much work to do!
What about Daniel?
He'll find us. Let's go!
READING GROUP
~TEEN~ FICTION
ALPHA BY AUTHOR
We need to start with the basics. Every book ever written about cool kids...

THE CLIQUE
THE HOUSE ON MANGO STREET
THE BABY-SITTERS CLUB
PRINCESS DIARIES
PRIDE AND PREDJUDICE
LORD OF THE FLIES
DIARY OF A WIMPY KID
HOLES
FREAKS, GEEKS, & COOL KIDS
FLOWERS FOR ALGERNON
SWEET VALLEY HIGH
UTHERING HEIGHTS
BOOK THIEF
STARGIRL
TWILIGHT
THE HOBBIT
ROMEO & JULIET
THE HATE U GIVE
THE OUTSIDERS

5:00 P.M.
I'm beat. How about we all go home and get some food?
We *have* food.
RINKLI CHIPS
Chips are *not* food.
You're probably right. We can't burn out on the first day. We have so much more to do!
Ugh.
How about we focus on what we *did* do?
THUD
It's not too bad. We got a lot done. But we still have to get all the info from all *those* books...
TEEN FICTION
PSYCHOLOGY
SOCIOLOGY
...and *those* books...

...into *there.*
Seriously?
Why can't *C.C.* read them?
I liked you better when you were refusing to do work in Coding Club.
That's not a bad idea. Instead of us reading the books and entering data, why don't we just have C.C. pull books from the internet?
Because C.C. can't tell a good source from a bad one.
Okay, so...we give a book our seal of approval and *then* he uploads a copy for analysis.
Tomorrow.
Later!
Bye!

THE NEXT DAY...
EMMA
AND THE NEXT...

THREE DAYS LATER
THROWBACK THURSDAY:
MEAN GIRLS
6:30 pm
Shhhhh!
DUDS
FRIDAY

I love this movie, but I don't get why Dionne is so mean all the time.

What do you mean?

I mean, does she like Tai or not? She always seems like she's mad at her.

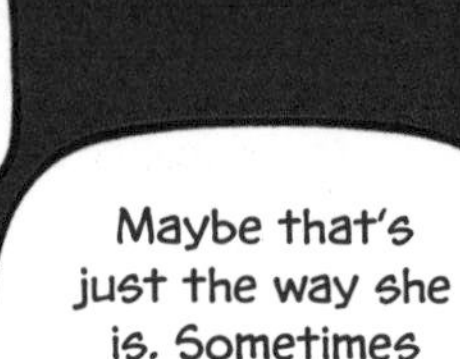

Maybe that's just the way she is. Sometimes people want to sound friendly but it just comes out wrong.

But I guess you're right... It does come across as kind of mean.

You know what? I take it back. I kinda like her the way she is.

TODAY IS:
NOVEMBER 6TH
TAP TAP TAP
TAP TAP T
BONK
HEHE
HAHA

AND THEN, ONE TUESDAY...
TAP TAP TAP TAP TAP TAP
TAP TAP TAP TAP
TAP TAP TAP
TAP TAP TAP
Pass me the next book.
There isn't one.
What do you mean?
I mean...

...we're out of books.
No. *Way.*
No, really... Look!
So, does that mean...
It means we're done with research. Phase one is complete. We begin phase two.
So...
Tomorrow morning. Let's meet before school.
PING!

Hi, sweet Pea! We got called in for a last minute meeting. We'll be home by 8.
Is everything okay?
What?
Oh—yeah. Everything's cool.
XX MOM

CHAPTER 8
PING!
good morning!!!
WHY DO YOU GET UP SO EARLY?
IT'S NOT SATURDAY!
hello?
What's up?
meet out front before school!
You could have told us that at ANY time that wasn't 6 a.m.
But okay!
see you there!
Are you ready for today?
Sure! I mean, I'm a little worried that it won't go well.
It's not supposed to go perfectly. This is the feedback round. If something gets screwed up, just make sure you let C.C. know what he did wrong.
I know, I just don't want him to screw up as much as he did before. I don't want you guys to have wasted all that time and have it not work out.

Hey. We *wanted* to waste our time.
I'm also kind of worried about embarrassing myself again. It's been nice to not have people think of me as the weird girl who talks to herself.
I know.
Well, I have something that will help with that.
RUSTLE
Ear buds?
Good ones. You won't have to talk nearly so loud for C.C. to hear you. And no one else will be able to hear him talking to you, either.
Thanks. Where'd you get them?
I had them at home. Just try not to lose them, okay?
Sure.

Thanks.
I really mean it.
Are you ready? Let's fire it up! Maybe we should start inside? Or should we just turn on the app here?
Whoa, slow down!

Sorry.
I'm just *so* excited.
Let's just turn on C.C. and see what happens!
Where are we?
What'd I miss?
POP!
CLICK
TAP
Oh. It's *these* two again.
TAP
TAP
TAP
It's 7:45 a.m. on Wednesday, C.C. Just a normal day at school.
Well, no one important to see here. Let's keep moving.
Maybe we should've spent some time improving his attitude.

See that group of girls?
Yeah...
We're going to go over there and make friends.
What?! You can't just walk into a group of popular kids and introduce yourself! Who *knows* what they might do?
I'm sorry. My preferences do not allow me to accept input from you.
Arggh!
Well, I did tell him to ignore you...
Listen. You could be an outcast for the rest of middle school—no, scratch that. *All the way through high school.*
The only way to find out if it's going to work is to try.

He's right, Morgan. That's the whole point of the beta test. We have to see how it works and *then* give feedback.
But didn't you already try this before? Remember the handshake incident?
Ahem.
Okay, that wasn't my best call. But this time, you have an "in."
I can't... I just can't watch this.
Well, maybe you shouldn't. I mean, I should probably do this by myself. To make sure the results aren't skewed.
Yeah, I guess that makes sense.
I'll report in at lunch.
I'll tell you what to say, you do the talking.

Hi! I'm *so* sorry for butting in on you like this, but I just *love* that necklace!
It's from blingshop, right? Their Save the Oceans collection?
Oh my God! How'd you know that? I *love* that collection. Everything you spend there goes directly to ocean conservation efforts.
That's so cool. It's *really* important to protect our oceans.
I totally agree. I went to an *amazing* seafaring summer camp this year—I want to be a marine biologist.

I'm Tanya, by the way.
I'm Anna...
Maria.
Your earrings are soooo cute. Where did you get them?

So, it worked?
It *totally* worked! Tanya invited me to go shopping with her this weekend!
Huh. That's pretty cool.
MUNCH MUNCH
I *guess* that's cool. If you like shopping.
Ummm... Oh yeah: in Social Studies, C.C. got me a better seat—so I won't get lost at the back of the class anymore.
Yeah, I did. I'm kind of awesome that way.
Any glitches?
Not yet.
It's smooth sailing from here on out, baby!
Hmph.

Morgan... are you okay? You seem a little–
A little like I worked for *weeks* on this app and then I got left out once things started to get good?
Is *that* what's bothering you?
What else would it be?
I don't know. I thought maybe–
What would you know?

Morgan...I'm really sorry you got left out of this stage of the testing. It's not that we didn't *want* you. It just turned out this way.
Yeah. No offense, but you're just a little too—
Enthusiastic. He was going to say *enthusiastic*.
Sure, let's go with that.
We just need C.C. to work without interference. Just for this week.
I'll give you updates at lunch every day, and I can tweak the program every night. After a couple of weeks, we can start working together again!
Sounds good to me.
Morgan?
Okay. A couple of weeks. For science and middle schoolers everywhere.

A COUPLE OF DAYS LATER
Zoey!
DAN CAN!
HAWTHORNE MIDDLE SCHOOL
Hey! Zoey!
PANT PANT

Zoey!
Oh, hey, Morgan!
SKID
I've been yelling forever!
HUFF HUFF
Sorry. I guess I couldn't hear you with the headphones.
PANT PANT
Why didn't you tell me, C.C.?
You told me to ignore input from her, remember?

SATURDAY
PING!
2:00 PM
SATURDAY, NOV 16
MORGAN SHU
how are things going with CC? anything new?
NEW TEXT MESSAGE
SHOVE

MONDAY
Over here!
To me!
Throw it this way!
See that kid with the broken glasses? He's quiet but likable. If you throw the ball to him, kids will assume you're being generous.
WHOOSH
Nice one!
Good catch!

ONE WEEK LATER
DT
MS
Coding Club meeting after school?
Definitely!
ZM
is it time?
Finished programming the new macros. Ready for reboot!
OMG!!! Cool Code 2.0!!!!!!!!
This is kind of a big moment.
Are you kidding me? This is a *huge* moment.
DAN CAN
Wait. C.C. isn't going to "ignore" my "input" anymore, is he?
Nope. We wiped all the preferences from C.C. 1.0.
Then I am *so excited!* Let's fire this thing up.
Wait. Don't you think *Zoey* should get to start the program? It's her baby, after all.
DAN CAN

Oh. Yeah! Go for it, Zoey.
Thanks, guys. Although I don't know if I'd call C.C. a baby. He's more like a bossy older brother...
PRESS THE BUTTON!
Okay. Sheesh.
Here goes.
TAP
30%
DOWNLOADING AI CORE...
50%
READING SLANG DICTIONARY INTO MEMORY...

This is kind of...
...anticlimactic?
60%
UPDATING INFLUENCER PROTOCOL...
Yeah.
Maybe we should get a snack?
I'm in!
CLINK
WHIRRR
CLUNK
MUNGH
MUNGH
MUNGH

Helllllllooo?

Welcome to the Cool Code. Who would you like to impress today?
THE COOL CODE
Whoa.
Yeah. Whoa.
DAN CAN

You really... blinged up the interface.
Heh heh.
I guess I got a little carried away. Is it too much?
Nah. It's perfect. It's like there's a party inside the computer.
Should we test it out?
Sure.
Let me just activate my profile.
CLICK
POP!
Hello! I'm C.C., your guide to the social world. What can I do for you today?

Nice! He's friendlier now!
Hi, C.C. I'm Zoey.
Zoey, I have your data on file. What social situation can I help you with?
Well, I'm new to this school, and... ummm...
I guess I want the other kids to think I'm cool.
I can help you with that.
How long have you been in attendance at your new school?
I guess, like, six weeks?
SIX WEEKS?! ARE YOU NUTS?!
Okay, so... not so much friendlier.

We don't have any time to waste. New kids have an advantage in establishing cool. No one knows about their past mistakes.
POOF
That's true.
But the first months are crucial. You have a very small window before your classmates make up their minds about you.
That also sounds right.
Of course it's right! Do you have any idea how big my database is?
Yeah. I do. Because I *built* it.
So... what should I do?
You need to go big.
Make a splash—do something that will get *everyone's* attention. Pull a massive prank. Star in a musical...

Okay, so–
What's that?
POOF!
What?
DAN CAN
That sticker you're wearing.
What's it for?
Oh!
I'm running for student council president.
DAN CAN
That's perfect.
You need to run for student council president, Zoey.
Uhhhh...

I can't run against Daniel.
Sure you can!
No. I can't. Daniel helped *program* C.C. He's my friend!
What? *This* guy?
C.C. and Daniel would be going head-to-head. It's the ultimate test! Can Daniel's creation beat him at his own game?
DAN CAN
You want to be popular? You need to do something bold. Something that shows you have a ton of confidence.
CRACK
POOF!
Me?

This is it. Take it or leave it.
POOF!
DAN CAN
Ugh. Fine.
I like Coding Club more than student council anyway.
DAN CAN
But if you win, you need to introduce some of my ideas to improve the school. Deal?
Okay. Deal.

Is everything okay back there? You look worried.
Yeah, I guess.
You *guess*? Hmmmm...
How was Coding Club?
It was pretty good. We got our new program running.
Really? That's such a great feeling!
Yeah, it is, but...
"But"?
We decided I'm going to run for student council president.

You decided *in Coding Club* to run for student council president?
Well, I think that's a great idea! Student government is a great way for you to meet lots of people...
I guess that's what I'm worried about.
Like I told you before: everyone is going to love you once they know you.
Dad, you just don't get it.
SLAM!
REMEMBER...
IT MIGHT TURN OUT OKAY
POOF
FLOP

CHAPTER 9
RIIINNNGGGG
TAP
YOU HAD ME TURNED OFF ALL NIGHT?
CLICK
VOL
CLICK
VOL
CLICK
VOL
CLICK
VOL
CLICK
VOL

You have so much to do! There's no time for sleep!
MUNCH
MUNCH
MUNCH
Step one: announce your candidacy.
Step two: form a committee.
No problem. Daniel and Morgan will help me.
Ummm...no. We're not trying to win an election. We're making you popular.
Step three: schmooze.
Lose the pin.

I'll start working on your platform.
Platform?
Hellooooo? Do you know *anything* about student government?
I guess not. I mean, I've never really been a student in a school before.
So, what? I talk about what I'll do if I'm elected?
If you want to win, yes. But *your* platform is going to be bait.
What's *that* supposed to mean?
You'll see.
I'm not sure this is worth it...

Whoa, whoa.
What. Is. *This?*
The bus. Are you glitching?
I am not glitching. And we are *not* getting on the bus.
We've been over this before.
That was the *old* C.C. The *new* C.C. is a finely calibrated system for cool and I WILL NOT RIDE THE BUS!!!

I guess I could get my scooter...
Are you in *kindergarten*? NO. You can skateboard.
I don't know *how* to skateboard.
It's three miles to school! I can't walk it in time.
Then be late.
POOF!

WAY, WAY, WAY LATER...
OFFICE
BAM!
Hey! Did you just get here? First period is almost over...
Are you okay? You look kind of—
Angry?
Tired. But angry, too.
That sounds about right.
I need the form to enter the student council race.
Oh! Right.
Thanks.
STUDENT COUNCIL FORM 1A:

How's it going with C.C.?
C.C.'s doing *great.*
BRRRIIINNG
Don't look so grumpy.
Say hi to that kid. His name is Carl.
Hi, Carl!
Hi, ummm... new kid.

Here comes Tanya.
H–
Don't say hi unless she says it first!
Hi, Zoey!
Okay, *now* turn around and pretend you didn't see her before.
Oh, hi, Tanya!

CLICK
Ugh. C.C. 1.0 has a lot to answer for. We'll deal with *your locker* after school.
AH BLAH BLAH
AH BLAH BL

Hey!
Say, "I wish I had one of those."
What? Why?
Just do it! Say it loud enough for the whole class to hear.
Ummm...
I wish I had one of those!
HAHAHAHAHAHAHAHAHA
What did I just say?
Don't worry about it. You killed it!

Your goal is to be seen by as many kids as possible during lunch. Do *not* sit down.
Zoey!
Hi, guys!
NO SITTING!
Whoa. Is it possible that C.C. has gotten even *more* pushy?
How's it going?

I'm crushing it.
I'll take feedback from the human, please.
He actually kind of is. But I wish we'd upgraded his personality.
Genius is rarely appreciated in its time.
That would've taken forever. Plus, I kind of like him. Gives me someone to argue with.
He's exhausting. He made me walk all the way to school this morning.
Is that why you were so late?
Yeah. Apparently he'll self-destruct if I take him on the bus. I can only walk or skateboard, and I don't have a skateboard, so...
You can borrow mine!
Thanks! But I don't know how to ride one...
PFFFFt! It's easy. I can totally teach you.

That would be–
Time's up!
But I–
No time! You need to move on to other kids.
Bye...
I guess.
Don't sweat it, kid. I can look up a skateboarding how-to for you.

BRIIINNNGG
That was fun!
But maybe next time I could actually, you know, have more time to *eat* at lunch.
GRUMBLE GRUMBLE
Maybe.
But don't count on it.

Good morning, Hawthorners! It's Wednesday!
blah blah blah
...and we have a late addition to the student council race. Zoey McIntyre will be running for student council president.
GULP
You're running for president?
Yes?
Cool!
Hmm...

Zoey!
I got your text!
But I didn't...
DOO DOO DOO
DOO DOO
Oh. Um... right.
I would *love* to be your campaign manager. Your ocean conservation ideas are amazing—especially the one about limiting plastic in the cafeteria.
This is going to be *sooooo* much fun.
Yay?

You sent a text without telling me?
Yep! Another home run.
You can't just pretend you're me and send out messages.
Why not?
Because people will think the messages are coming from me. They should say things that *I* think.
You don't think we should make changes to benefit the oceans?
No.
I mean yes. But that's not the point!
Look. You didn't know any of the things you said to Tanya about blingshop when you first met her. You have absolutely no interest in student council. And you still have no idea what you said that was so funny in second period. How is this any different?
It's...
Because...
It just *is*. Okay?
Sheesh. Okay. Preference saved.

I DON'T KNOW WHY IT FREAKS ME OUT SO MUCH THAT C.C. WAS SENDING TEXTS. I GUESS I KIND OF FEEL LIKE A FAKE. I MEAN, PASSING OFF SOMEONE—SOME*THING*—ELSE'S IDEAS AS MY OWN JUST FEELS SO...DISHONEST.
BUT I MADE C.C. SO DOES THAT MEAN THAT HIS IDEAS ARE MINE, TOO?
I'm so excited to run your campaign. *Everybody* wants to join. We're having a "Go for Zo!" meeting after school today.
We are?
Mr. Asher says we can use his room. See you there!
Um...bye?
What is happening?
You asked Tanya to run your campaign?

C.C. did. He didn't even ask me.
That's right!
Oh. Okay.
But I guess it's a good idea, right?
Sure.
Um, I just remembered I have to go get something out of my locker.
Okay... See you later, I guess?

SIGH
TAP TAP TAP TAP
I have to stay late for a meeting. Can you pick me up at 4:30?
ZM
See you after school!
Are you going to the "Go For Zo" meeting?
Isn't everybody?
GULP

2:55 P.M.
RUMBLE
RUMBLE
SWOOSH
CLACK

BLAH
BLAH
BLAH
MURMUR
MURMUR
BLAH
HAHAHAHA
GIGGLE
You need to take charge of this meeting.

Right.
Guys! Hello? Everyone!
Not like that. Take *charge.*
Climb up on that desk and hold up your phone.
FWEEEEE!!!
HEY! Zoey's up here!
Start talking, kid. Don't use too many question marks.

COUGH
COUGH
Just introduce yourself. They know who you are, but it makes you look humble.
Hi. I don't think I know all of you yet, but I'm Zoey—
Ahem!
Oh! Should I get off the desk?

You should.
But that's not why I'm here.
There's a whole stack of *pizzas* in the school office for you.
I didn't order any pizzas—
Yes, you did.
I did?
I did.
Okay then, I guess I should go get them.
Stay here.
Or not. I guess I should stay here and keep the meeting going...

I'll get 'em.
Okay, so... thank you for coming to the meeting. As you know, I'm running for class president on a Save the Oceans platform...
BLAH BLAH BLAH
BLAH BLAH BLAH BLAH BLAH
I'm so grateful that you are all interested in helping out.
I'm gonna need a little help with carrying.

Tanya is going to be my campaign manager, so maybe she should talk for a bit.
No problem.
Ummm... gonna need *more* help than just you.
TICK TICK TICK
PIZZA PIZZA
THANK YOU
THANK YOU

Did someone call for pizza?
PIZZA PIZZA
Apparently so...
Where did all this come from?
I ordered it.
But how did you pay for it?
I used your dad's credit card.

WHAT?!
My program is housed on your parents' server, remember? I just did a little look-see and found their financial info. No problem.
Time to take this up a notch!

4:15 P.M.
That. Was. Awesome!
Yeah...Zoey's actually pretty cool.
Doo doo doooooo. Yeah! That was an unmitigated success!
How are we going to get this cleaned up?
You're on your own there, kid. Cleanup is for people with bodies.

IF YOU WANT TO PROGRAM A COMPUTER TO DO SOMETHING, YOU HAVE TO BREAK DOWN THAT TASK INTO ITS MOST BASIC STEPS. FORWARD, TURN, STOP. IF THIS, THEN THAT.
SOMETIMES YOU HAVE TO DO THE SAME THING IN THE REAL WORLD. PICK UP. SWEEP. DUMP. YOU CAN BREAK DOWN PRETTY MUCH ANY TASK AND GET IT DONE.
THAT DOESN'T MEAN IT'S GOING TO BE FUN.

MORGAN
for ZO

Great meeting, Zoey. You're going to be an awesome president.
What? Oh, thanks...
I have to stay late for a meeting. Can you pick me up at 4:30?
TAP TAP TAP TAP TAP TAP TAP TAP TAP TAP
I have to stay late for a meeting. Can you pick me up at 4:30?
My meeting is over. Are you guys coming to pick me up?
ZM
And... I can explain about the pizza.
ZM

I'm home!

Did something happen? Where were–
Oh–hi, hon! How was school?
You're just sitting here working? Did you even *notice* I wasn't on the bus?
Unbelievable.

I've accessed 37 different tutorials on skateboarding and accumulated the top tips for learning to ride. The physics are simple. Keep your center of gravity low and over the board.
Oh, thanks. That totally clears it up.
Searching...
How's this? Bend your knees but keep your body upright.
Okay. Yeah. I can do that.

CHAPTER 10

DECEMBER 5
GO WITH ZO
GO WITH ZO

DECEMBER 10
GO WITH ZO
GO WITH ZO
DAN CAN!
GO WITH ZO
DAN CAN!
MEET THE CANDIDATE:
ZOEY MCINTYRE

DECEMBER 12
Damon! Awesome win last night!
Hey, Michael, how's your grandma?
OMG, Raven! Did you *hear* that new K-pop song?!
Lainie! The mathletes are really kicking butt this month!
Whoa! *Love* that outfit!
BUMP

SHOOOOSH
RUMBLE
RUMBLE
CRASH

IT CAN'T BE MORNING ALREADY, CAN IT?
Zoey?
Zoey! You need to leave for school in 10 minutes.
SNAP!
be cool.

HUFF
HUFF
I can't *believe* you left me behind. What were you thinking?
You know you can't do this without me. Right? *I'm* the mastermind.
Hey, Zoey!
Zoey, over here!
Look at these kids. *None* of them would even know your name if it wasn't for me.

THE DREADED LUNCH. AGAIN.
What are your vegan options today?
Forgot your lunch?
Morgan! Hi!
I got up late. I'm *so* tired.
C.C. has me running around all day, every day.
You bet! You can't make friends sitting still.

That doesn't sound right...
I'm a state-of-the-art computer program. I don't make mistakes.
That's *definitely* not right.
I'm sorry I've been so busy.
It's not a big deal. We've been really busy too.
Right, Daniel?
What?
Oh! Hey, Zoey!
I've been helping Daniel with his campaign.

Okay, great. I just didn't want you to think I was avoiding you.
You're not avoiding us. You're testing out our app.
Ahem.
Yeah. That's what you're supposed to be doing.
POOF!
EXCUSE ME!
What?
I have new information.
Okay...

I have completed an analysis of the relative coolness of the entire Hawthorne School eighth-grade class.
I didn't ask you to do that.
You don't ask me to do anything. I independently collect and analyze data to determine the optimal course of action at any point in time. This is no different.
It really is an incredibly impressive program, Zoey.
So at this moment in time you need to know how cool every person in the school is?
Not the whole school. Just the eighth grade.
It's a separate project that I've been working on since I was rebooted.

It took you a *week* to process?
Yeah—what took you so long?
This school doesn't have a searchable database of all its students. It's disgraceful.
Yeah—someone should really build one.
Do I have your attention?
Um...yes?
First, I compiled a list of all of the eighth-grade students. Then, I observed each one when I encountered them during the day.

ADAM RODRIGUEZ
OVERALL ASSESSMENT: 70
CONVERSATIONAL SKILL 40
ATHLETIC ABILITY 60
KNOWN ASSOCIATES 84
JE NE SAIS QUOI 75
SMACK
I assigned each individual a score according to their objectively cool characteristics combined with their popularity with other kids in the school.
I don't know about this...
ADAM RODRIGUEZ
I ordered them according to their scores. There are 213 students in the eighth grade. It is unproductive for you to hang out with any student who ranks below #60 on the scale. These kids will make you seem less cool by association.
I'm not sure I really want to know this, but...what's my rank?
You're not included. Your rank is currently rising. I estimate that you will reach #1 by Christmas break.
Total success!

18 SAMANTHA JONES
19 CHLOE MILLER
20 TOMMY BALL
21 CONNOR BROWN
22 DANIEL THOMPSON
23 JENNY GARCIA
Daniel scored #22 in the ranking. He is useful to you as you pursue your goal.
THWACK
What's my score?
You are #183 in the ranking. As such, Zoey may not spend time with you.
C.C.! You can't say things like that. People have *feelings.*
I *like* spending time with Morgan.
No. It's okay.

He's a computer program. He's just telling it like it is.
But–
You should...go sit somewhere else or something.
You can't give up on the project now. We have to see how it works out.
Daniel?
I don't know, Zo. We *have* put a lot of time into it. But...
No buts. Get lost.
It's just for now. We'll hang out after, right?
Yeah. Sure.
Okay.

AND THEN: THIS HAPPENS.
TAP TAP TAP TAP TAP TAP TAP TAP TAP TAP TAP TAP
POKE POKE
CHEW
CRUNCH CRUNCH
TAP TAP TAP TAP
Is everything okay, Zo?
Yep. I'm fine.
SHOVE SHOVE

Can I be excused? I have a ton of homework.
Sure, hon. Don't work *too* hard.
You're one to talk.
SLAM!
BEE-YOU TIFUL
REMEMBER...
TOMORROW IS A NEW DAY

Liar. You are far from fine.
POP!
I'm *not* a liar.
POP!
Yes. You. Are.
I'm perfectly fine.
Then you're lying to yourself. Either way: liar.
Cool people are assertive, Zoey. They say what they mean.

You want me to be more assertive?
Obviously.
HOW'S THIS?!
I'M NOT FINE! AND IF YOU WOULD JUST STOP WORKING FOR ONE SECOND, YOU WOULD KNOW THAT.
SLAM!

Zoey?
Do you want to talk about it?
No.
I know Dad and I have been working too much lately.
SCHWICK SCHWICK
There's just so much to do. There's all the regular programming work that we have to finish...
...but there's also a lot of organizational stuff to take care of. It's just a lot.

I don't want you to think that we don't *want* to spend time with you. I miss our school days together... Family game nights...even just watching TV with you.
It's just... sometimes projects can have a life of their own. They start out as simple ideas, but they grow and grow until there isn't room for anything else.
SCHWICK SCHWICK
Does that make any sense? Maybe one day when you're older...
It makes sense now.
It does?
Yeah. I get it.
FLIP
MORGAN
Well, it's no excuse for us not being there when you need us. People are more important than projects.
I'm sorry.
Thanks, Mom.
MORGAN

So, tell me what's going on with you. How's school?
It's okay, I guess. There's so much going on.
You have a lot of work. I didn't think Hawthorne was going to be this challenging.
The schoolwork's actually not bad. It's the other stuff that's intense. Coding Club and the student council election...
SNIFF SNIFF
I guess I just really, really wanted to make friends, and I bit off more than I could chew.
Making friends *is* important. But you shouldn't have to work so hard to impress people. You're pretty great just the way you are.
Ugh, Mom. You sound just like Dad.
Haha! Okay. How about this?
You know what's important to you. Just make sure that those things are first on the list, and everything else will fall into place.

CHAPTER 11
REMEMBER...
♡ YOU'RE THE BOSS!
CLICK
CLICK
CLICK
PING!
THE NEXT DAY
REALLY SORRY ABOUT THE PIZZA ♡ Zo
Coding Club today?
DT
definitely! LOTS to talk about!
ZM
k
MS
Cool. See you after school.
DT
MUSIC TO CODE TO
ZO'S FUNKY VIBES
DAD'S OLD STUFF

GO WITH ZO
DAN GAN!
HAHAHAHAHAHAHA

BRIIIINGGG
I only had to correct you 19 times today. That's a total of 23 fewer cool errors than your average day last week.
At this rate, you'll hardly need any correction in another couple of weeks.
Of course, you will always need *some* level of guidance. A human can't begin to approximate my processing levels.
Wait a second. This isn't the way out of school.

Where are you going?
Oh, *no* you don't. You are *not* going to Coding Club.
Coding Club is *not* a cool activity. If just one of the other kids finds out that you're spending your free time coding and hanging out with #183, all bets are off.
Zoey, you have to make a decision. Do you want to be cool? Or do you want to hang out with these weirdos?
Hey! I thought I was #22?

Your cool rank changes constantly. I downgraded you to #31 based on that shirt.
SNICKER SNICKER
What do you guys think? Should we start the meeting?
Zoey, this is an extremely foolish course of action.
Sure. Who wants to go first?
I have an update.
Oh, do tell!
I think our program is a complete success. We should celebrate.

But we didn't even get to the election. Don't we need to know who wins?
Nope. C.C. said it himself—it wasn't about winning the election, it was about making me popular. And I'm definitely more popular than I would've been on my own. I think the program works.
Pfffft. You're only #8. You have a loooooong way to go.
I think we've done a great job. It's time to end the trial.
What?!
Are you sure about this?
I'm very sure.
Hey, wait a second!
Morgan, do you want to do the honors?
YES!

If you give up on me now, it's all over. You won't get a second chance at being the cool new kid. You'll just be one of the regular kids everyone already knows. With your skills, you'll never get above #100 in the ranking again.
Do it.
But–
CLICK
SQUEEEEEE!
POP!

So what do we do now?
I *definitely* need to get out of the student council race.
You know it's a lock, right? Adam did a poll and you beat me by 10 points.
Yeah. But you'll definitely make a better president.
So what are we going to do next?
If we hustle, we could still get that PTA database ready this semester...
Ugh. You know what? I'm in a good mood. Let's do it.
But it can wait till tomorrow, right? How about we celebrate today?

Okay, but we really need to get going on this project soon...
It can wait.
Great. 'Cause I could really use some lessons.
Awesome!
CLICK
THORNE MIDDLE SCHOOL

SATURDAY
I GUESS MOM WAS RIGHT: IT'S EASY TO LET WORK TAKE OVER YOUR LIFE. BUT AT THE END OF THE DAY, CODE ISN'T GOING TO LAUGH AT YOUR JOKES, SCARF SUNDAES AND WATCH MOVIES, OR UNDERSTAND HOW IT FEELS TO WIPE OUT IN THE CAFETERIA.
PING!
FOR THAT, YOU NEED FRIENDS. REAL-LIFE FRIENDS.
DT
Ready?
MS
IT'S SATURDAY!!!!!!!!
So? This data isn't going to upload itself.
DT
Meet me at the library at noon.
you're the worst
MS
but okay
TAP TAP TAP
C u there!
ZM
SURE, FRIENDSHIP CAN BE MESSY. PEOPLE ARE UNPREDICTABLE.

BUT MAYBE THAT'S WHAT MAKES IT ALL WORTHWHILE.